D0263731

RED FOX READ ALONE

It takes a special book to be a
RED FOX READ ALONE!

If you enjoy this book, why not
choose another READ ALONE
from the list?

Lindsay Camp
illustrated by Tony Ross

RED FOX

A Red Fox Book

Published by The Random House Group Ltd
20 Vauxhall Bridge Road, London, SW1V 2SA

A division of The Random House Group Ltd
London Melbourne Sydney Auckland
Johannesburg and agencies throughout the world

3 5 7 9 10 8 6 4 2

First published by Andersen Press Limited 1994
Red Fox edition 1995

This Red Fox edition 1999

Printed and bound in Great Britain by
Cox & Wyman Limited, Reading, Berkshire

Papers used by Random House UK Limited are natural, recyclable products
made from wood grown in sustainable forests. The manufacturing processes
conform to the environmental regulations of the country of origin.

RANDOM HOUSE UK Limited Reg. No. 954009

www.randomhouse.co.uk

ISBN 0 09 940223 8

Contents

1
Game Crazy

Emma was crazy about computer games.

She played them at school on the class computer. She played them at home on her mum's computer.

And when her mum was using her computer, Emma went round the corner to her best friend Rebecca's, and played games on her television set.

Emma's mum and dad used to moan about it all the time.

'Why don't you play your recorder instead?' said her mum. 'You were getting so good before you stopped practising.'

'Don't feel like it,' said Emma.

'Or you could draw a picture,' said her dad.

'Or read a book,' said her mum.

'Or take your bike out on the
pavement,' said her dad.

'No thanks,' said Emma. 'Computer
games are more exciting.'

2
The MiniMax

Then, just after Emma's birthday, her
Uncle Richard came to stay.

He'd just come back from America,
and he brought her the most fantastic
present.

It was a MiniMax Double-X
Personal Entertainment System.

It was small enough to take anywhere. It had earphones, so you could hear all kinds of exciting noises. And it came with three different games: Wobblyworld, The Evil Thargons, and Cabbages from Outer Space.

'Wow!' said Emma, rushing up to her room to experiment with it.

The first game she tried was
Cabbages from Outer Space. It was
brilliant.

She played it before she got out of
bed in the morning.

She played it in the bathroom,

and while she was having her breakfast.

She played it on the way to school,
and on the way home.

She played it when she went to the
supermarket with her dad,

and when she went to her
grandparents' house for tea.

In fact, the only times she didn't play
it were when she was in class, and
when she was asleep.

And then she dreamed about it.

Emma's parents moaned even more.

'You can't play with that thing all
the time,' said her dad.

'I said you can't play with that thing
all the time,' he repeated, pulling up
Emma's earphones so she would hear
him.

'Why not?' said Emma.

'Because there are so many better things to do in life,' said her mum.

'Not in my life there aren't,' said Emma. 'Computer games are more exciting than anything that ever happens to me.'

And she clamped her earphones firmly back on.

3
Level One

After school that day, Emma went round to Rebecca's house.

It was a beautiful sunny afternoon, and they played for quite a while in the tree-house that Rebecca's mum and dad had built in the garden.

Then they went inside to play
computer games on the television set.

'I was just going to bring you a snack
in the tree-house,' said Rebecca's mum.
But the girls didn't even hear her.

Soon, it was time for Emma to go home for supper. It was only a couple of minutes' walk, but she turned on her MiniMax anyway.

She hadn't played Cabbages from Outer Space since before school.

As she kicked Rebecca's front gate closed behind her, Emma was on Level 1.

She was concentrating so hard on
steering the space shuttle through the
asteroid shower that she didn't look up
from her screen for a second.

And with the sound turned up loud,
she didn't hear anything strange
either.

4
Level Two

Level 2 was harder, so Emma leaned against a lamp-post for a moment to make sure her hands were steady.

ARE YOU CERTAIN 'TIS SHE?
CERTAIN, CAPTAIN.
THEN WOBBLE HER ABOARD, MR MATE.

Emma had arrived at Ultra-
Galactica now so she needed to grab
a Cosmic Cabbage from the planet's
surface, using the Laser Lassoo.

Suddenly, Emma felt a very strange feeling – a sort of quiver-y shaking feeling, starting in her tummy and then spreading all over her body . . . but, yes, she'd got the cabbage.

'Bleepety-bleep, bleepety bleeepety-BLEEEEP!' went the MiniMax.

Emma was onto Level 3.

5
Level Three

Emma knew her mum would be cross if she was late for supper.

But she had to stop Captain Urg and his Space Pirates from boarding the shuttle and capturing the Cosmic Cabbage, so it was hard to hurry . . .

Captain Urg was getting closer.
Emma dodged – first to the left, then
to the right.

It was very strange, but suddenly her feet felt heavy, almost as if they were stuck to the ground . . .

With one last twist, Emma left Urg
and his space bandits behind.

Bleepa-bleepa bleep, buh-buh-buh
bleeeeep! She was onto Level 4.

PREPARE A THRONE FOR HER UNWOBBLINESS – AND PLOT A COURSE FOR THE PLANET JELLOID.
FULL **WIB-POWER**, SIR,
PRAY, A MOMENT, SIR. A LARGE CRAFT APPROACHES. I LIKE ITS APPEARANCE NOT...
THE **THARGONS**! THEY HAVE FOLLOWED US, AND NOW PREPARE AN AMBUSH!
WE MUST PROTECT THE PRINCESS!
STAND BY TO ACTIVATE **ULTRA WOBBLE...**

6
Level Four

Emma had landed safely on Urgold VI.
Now the game started to get really
difficult. And to make things even
harder, everything seemed to be
shaking up and down.

Emma wondered if it could be an
earthquake in Laburnum Drive, but
she wasn't going to look up at a
moment like this . . .

Emma clung on to the MiniMax's
controls as tightly as she could.

Now she had to send a search party
to the Carcassadian Caves to hunt for
the Sonic Shredder, while using her
foot-soldiers to guard the Cosmic
Cabbage from Urgold Super-
Caterpillars.

It needed maximum concentration.

The shaking was getting worse. It
must definitely be an earthquake,
thought Emma.

And she knew she should run home
to make sure her family were all right.
But she couldn't stop playing now –
not just when she was about to find
the Sonic Shredder . . .

7
Level Five

The earthquake seemed to be over –
and Emma had the Sonic Shredder.

She'd only reached Level 5 twice
before. Her hands trembled with
excitement.

If she could just shred the Cosmic
Cabbage fast enough . . .

THARGON SHIP ONLY HALF A WIB AWAY, SIR.
WE'RE LOST... UNLESS THE PINK PRINCESS CAN SAVE US!
SEE HOW SHE SEARCHES IN HER BOX FOR A SPELL TO SMITE THE THARGONS!

Emma finished shredding the first quarter of the cabbage.

'Yes!' she cried aloud – and then she remembered that she was in Laburnum Drive, and hoped that no one had heard her.

But she wasn't going to look up from her screen, not with three-quarters of the cabbage left to shred.

'Yes!' shouted Emma again, as she finished shredding the second quarter . . .

50

The third quarter was done. And
once more, Emma felt the strange
quiver-y feeling inside.

Her legs went all wobbly too – but
then, they always did when she was
really excited.

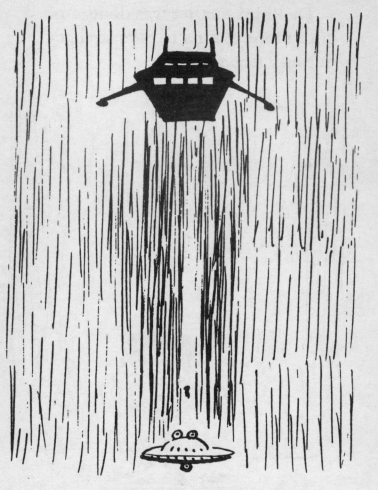

Emma finished shredding.

Bleep blip–blip–blip bleep bleep
bleeeeeep! The MiniMax played a
fanfare.

Emma had done it! She'd made the Cosmic Coleslaw, just in time.

She was onto Level 6.

She was so delighted she leapt high into the air . . .

8
Level Six

Now all Emma had to do was feed the
Cosmic Coleslaw to the Good Wizard
Warburton, to restore his faded
powers, and the Universe would be
saved.

Suddenly, she felt an even stranger
feeling than before – a sort of rushing,
whizzing, trembly, falling-to-pieces
feeling – but nothing was going to stop
her now.

One spoonful . . . two spoonfuls . . .
the strange feeling seemed to have
passed . . . three spoonfuls . . . Wizard
Warburton had finished all the
Cosmic Coleslaw.

Bleepety bleepety bleep bleep
bleepety blip-blip blippa-blippa
bleeeeeeeeeeep! The MiniMax went
mad. Wizard Warburton's powers
returned, and the Universe was safe.

Emma had scored the maximum
possible.

She knew she should be pleased, but the funny thing was she felt a little disappointed.

What was she going to do now?

She supposed she could try playing Wobblyworld or The Evil Thargons instead – but somehow she felt as if she already knew what they would be like. It was almost as if she had played them before . . .

Emma looked up from her screen, and saw she was right outside her own front door.

To her relief, the house didn't seem to have been damaged by the earthquake.

She pulled off her earphones and hurried up the path, hoping she wasn't too late for supper.

That night, going upstairs to say
goodnight to Emma, her mum heard
a strange noise coming from her room.
It wasn't the usual bleep-bleep-
bleepety-bleeping of the MiniMax . . .

As her mum came into the room, Emma put her recorder under her pillow and snuggled down ready for sleep.

Her mum sat down on the edge of the bed.

'Mum,' said Emma, 'do you know what I did today on the way home from Rebecca's?'

'No,' said her mum, kissing her. 'What?'

'I saved the Universe,' said Emma.

'You and that machine,' said her mum, smiling.

'Do you think you and dad could build me a tree-house like Rebecca's?' said Emma.